Sand, Sea & Tamburello
10 humorous and heartwarming short stories for Summer

Stefania Hartley

THE*SICILIAN*MAMA

To Sandy: friend, editor and all-round wonderful person. x

CONTENTS

1. FISHFUL THINKING

Rosetta, the doctor's daughter, had the most beautiful hair in the village. When she sat at her balcony to dry it in the sun, it shone like spun gold.

Wash, comb and dry in the sun. Every morning she did the same thing.

"It's not good for your hair to be washed so much," her mother told her.

But Rosetta didn't care about her hair. All she cared about was being at her balcony when the young fishmonger drove past in his three-wheeled Piaggio Ape.

He peddled his wares through the Ape's loudspeaker in a velvety tenor voice.

"Swordfish, mullet, brill and eel—only ten euros: a wonderful deal!"

Every morning, he stopped under Rosetta's balcony and looked up at her with his jade eyes sparkling against his golden skin. Rosetta's heart skipped a beat.

"Would you like some fish today, *signorina*?"

"No, thank you."

She shook her head, making her hair glitter in the sun.

"Your hair blinds me."

"Then don't look."

"I can't help it. I am like the fish when they swim up to the lights of the fishing boats at night."

"Be careful, because the fish end up in the net," Rosetta warned him.

"This fish wants to get caught in this net," he replied, his hands on his heart.

"You shouldn't talk like this to girls on their balconies," she protested at this point, because she knew that the neighbours were listening behind their shutters.

She retreated behind her French doors.

But she kept looking at his Ape through the slats until it disappeared from her street. She would have loved to go downstairs and buy his fish, to be closer to him.

But her parents didn't like fish and her mother said it made the house smell. So all she could do was entertain conversations with him from her balcony, every morning a little longer, every time a little deeper.

He never seemed in a hurry to drive on, and

they talked about the iridescent fish and the green sea where it came from, the parched mountains behind the village and the cobalt blue sky above it.

One afternoon, when Rosetta was trying to concentrate on her poetry book, her sister asked her, "Don't you like poetry anymore?"

"I do, but I've met a better poet than the ones in the books."

"Who would that be?"

"The young fishmonger who drives past our house every morning."

"If you marry a fishmonger, your house will smell of fish forever," her sister pointed out.

"I don't care."

Rosetta had seen how gently he handled the fish and had imagined him holding their babies. She had heard him sing the praises of his fish with the voice of an angel and had imagined him singing a love song for her. What if his house, his clothes and his bed smelled of fish? If that was the smell of his skin, it would smell delicious to her.

"He's poor."

"I don't mind," she insisted.

If the only gold he ever possessed was the golden speckles in his eyes, and the only silver he owned the scales of his fish, she would be the richest woman on earth.

"Mamma and Papà will never allow it."

This was the only thing that saddened her.

***

Like every morning, Turi drove his Ape down the village's main road. He didn't have many customers here, and the sensible thing to do would be to skip this village and use his fuel and time somewhere else. But he had stopped being sensible the moment he had clapped eyes on the girl on the balcony.

"Tuna, mackerel, squid and bream! I fulfil your every dream," he sang.

She was his dream.

He stopped under her balcony and sang into the loudspeaker.

"Octopus, shrimps, clams and prawn, each of your wishes is my very own."

He stepped out of the Ape and looked up. There she was, beautiful like the sun in a cloudless sky.

"You can't possibly fulfil people's dreams," she challenged him, working her comb through her hair.

"Try me."

"How do you know what other people wish for?"

"I can tell. First of all, I need to know their names. What's yours?"

"Rosetta."

"And I'm Turi. Now I've fulfilled our first wishes—we know each other's names."

"I didn't want to know your name," Rosetta protested, but her cheeks turned the colour of lobster shells.

"If you want me to fulfil more wishes, you'll need my fish," Turi continued.

"I knew it was just a trick."

She busied herself with an imaginary knot in her hair.

"It's not a trick: it's my song's promise. And I didn't say that you need to buy my fish," he explained. "I'm going to give it to you for free."

"Why would you do that?"

"Because this is a trick." He picked his biggest bream, round and silver like the moon, and dropped it into a paper cone for her. It would be enough for her whole family. "If your parents like it, you'll start buying my fish."

And he hoped that they might like him too.

"My mamma doesn't allow fish to be cooked in the house because of the smell."

"Then I'll cook it and bring it to you tonight."

The girl looked flustered.

"That can't be done."

"Why not?"

"Because… bream has bones that get stuck in people's throats," she improvised.

"Then I'll bring you a lobster."

"Lobsters have sharp pinchers and they're hard to get into."

"How about an octopus?"

"Octopuses have many arms, like unfaithful people."

"Then an eel."

"Eels are slippery, like deceitful people."

Turi wasn't put off.

"Then you should have my swordfish."

"Swords are for war, not for the table."

"Tuna, then. Flavoursome and red like the heart."

She didn't protest.

"What time do you have your supper?" he asked.

"Eight o'clock. But I don't think it's a good idea."

"Your family will love it."

The rest of the morning, Turi couldn't concentrate. When someone asked for a mullet, he gave them shrimps, and a few times he forgot to take payment. He finished his round earlier than usual and dropped by the greengrocer to buy some tomatoes and a sprig of mint.

Back home, he took a large chunk of tuna, made holes with his fingers and pushed salt, black pepper and mint leaves into every hole.

Then he heated olive oil in a pan and sealed the tuna before making a sauce with the tomatoes, some garlic and some chilli pepper. When everything was ready, he transferred it into his best serving dish, covered it with his whitest towel and set off to Rosetta's village. Thankfully, the Sicilian dish of *tonno ammuttunato* was just as nice cold as it was warm.

***

"Rosetta, are you coming to supper?" her mother called from the dining room.

Rosetta was at the front door, peering into the road in search of a familiar Ape. Maybe Turi had been joking earlier. She was about to close the door when his Ape chugged into her road.

"Just a minute, Mamma," she called back, stepping out just as he unfolded himself from the Ape's cab.

She had always seen him from high up, and now that she was eye level with him, her knees buckled a little.

"I've got to go; Mamma has called for supper."

"Then I'm just in time."

Turi handed her a dish wrapped in a teacloth.

"Thank you."

As he smiled and tipped his head goodbye, he took with him another little piece of her heart.

Her family weren't impressed.

"You know that we don't eat fish," her mother complained.

"A doctor's daughter cannot date a fishmonger," her father added. "We don't want you to see him again."

Nobody touched the fishmonger's dish. When everyone had gone to bed, Rosetta tried it secretly. It was delicious.

***

Turi didn't sleep that night. How had Rosetta's family received his dish? How had they received him?

As he drove his Ape down their road, he searched Rosetta's balcony with his gaze.

"Today's special is grey mullet, a fine delicacy for your gullet! And if you try my amberjack, you'll be surely coming back!"

Rosetta wasn't at her balcony. Had he been too forward?

Just as he was about to drive on, her front door opened and she appeared. Her smile was tinged with sadness. He stopped the Ape and leapt out.

"Hello."

"Thank you for the tuna," she said, thrusting

the clean dish and the cloth into his hands.

"Did you like it?"

"I loved it."

"What about your parents?"

"They didn't want to try it." She averted his gaze. "I'm not allowed to dry my hair on the balcony anymore."

"That's a shame. I'm sorry."

Was he ever going to see her again? If only he hadn't brought them that tuna dish.

"This afternoon I'm riding my bicycle to the beach," she told him with a smile.

It was an invitation!

"What a coincidence. I have to collect some fish from the harbour this afternoon," he lied.

The harbour was next to the beach, and the date was fixed.

**

That summer went in a whirlwind of bliss. Every afternoon, Rosetta rode her bicycle to the beach and Turi met her there with his Ape. They sat on the sand, watching the waves and talking about underwater prairies of seagrass in bloom, fish that looked like rocks and rocks that looked like fish. And they fell deeper and deeper in love.

"In September I'm going to Palermo to study at the university," she told him one day.

"I'll be here, waiting for you," he promised.

***

At the university, Rosetta studied hard, went to parties and met many eligible young men, but her heart was back at home with Turi. Every time she came back for the holidays, they met at the beach, come rain or shine.

"Haven't you got that fishmonger out of your head yet?" her sister asked her.

"No. I love him."

"You are about to become a doctor and he's a fishmonger," her father warned her when he found out. "It will never work."

"I love him, Papà."

When she graduated and came home, she invited her family to the beach for a celebratory swim.

They were treading the shallows, enjoying the coolness of the water, when her father yelped in pain.

Rosetta and her sister helped him out of the water and sat him on the sand, then Rosetta inspected the hurting foot. There wasn't any sign of a wound, so her father couldn't have stepped on broken glass. Nor did it feel like a cramp. Neither father nor daughter could come up with a diagnosis or a cure.

"You must have stepped on a stonefish."

It was Turi's voice, strong and confident, and he was coming towards them with a bucket.

He explained that stonefish have a venomous spike on their dorsal fin, and that heat inactivates the venom.

The two doctors had never had a personal encounter with the fish before, and swimmers who got stung didn't usually go to the doctor.

Turi poured some hot water from the bucket onto her father's foot and it immediately was better.

Rosetta's father admitted that Turi might not have a medical degree, but he was a good and capable man.

***

That afternoon, in front of a beautiful green and blue sea, Turi went down on one knee and asked Rosetta to marry him.

She said yes, and his heart jumped out of his chest like a flying fish. He put a ring of pearls and corals on her finger and kissed her. They sat on the beach holding hands, and her hair glittered like gold.

"Do you remember when I said you couldn't fulfil people's dreams?" she said.

He smiled at the memory.

"Yes."

"I was wrong." She smiled. "You just have."

2. NO STONE UNTURNED

Tanino and Melina had only one granddaughter, and Melina often felt like she wasn't enough for the two of them to share, let alone to share with Valentina's other grandparents.

Now that Sicilian schools had broken up for the summer and Valentina needed childminding, which set of grandparents should have her for three days a week and which for two?

Melina laid some hazelnut spread and ricotta over a bed of shortcrust to make a crostata for tomorrow, when it would be their turn to have Valentina for the day.

"We should have Valentina three days a week. We live closest to her," she said to Tanino, who was stooped over his crossword at the kitchen table.

"Perhaps because we see her every day anyway, the other grandparents should have her the extra day," Tanino returned without lifting his gaze from his crossword.

"Oh, really? Whose side are you on?" Melina demanded.

"I didn't realise there were sides," Tanino replied calmly.

"It's not fair. We only have one grandchild while her other *nonni* have seven—one for every day of the week. They don't need to have Valentina at all!"

Melina laid strips of shortcrust over the crostata like the bars of a cage.

Tanino finally lifted his gaze from his crossword and looked at her pointedly.

"How do you spell 'jealousy'?"

***

The next morning, Melina's crostata was just out of the oven and cooling on the kitchen table when Valentina was dropped off.

Tanino was still in bed, but Melina had been up since six to bake.

"What did you do with your other nonni yesterday?" Melina asked her granddaughter as soon as they sat for breakfast.

Valentina's face lit up.

"We went to the beach! It was so much fun. We built sandcastles and played in the water. Can we go to the beach today?" Valentina asked.

A trip to the beach usually required days of preparation. But if the other nonni had given Valentina such a fun day, she and Tanino must do even better.

"Of course!" Melina agreed. "I'll just tell your *nonno*."

***

Tanino was sitting in his favourite café with friends. "Take us to the beach, Tanino," his friends demanded.

"Don't you know that I hate the beach?" Tanino replied, but as soon as he'd said it the café's floor tiles crumbled into a fine sand.

The legs of his chair were sinking in.

"Help!" he cried and awoke with a start.

Melina was shaking him.

"Finally!" she exclaimed. "Quick, get up. We must go to the beach."

"We can't…" he mumbled, trying to keep his eyes open.

"Valentina went to the beach with her other nonni yesterday," Melina said, as if that was all the explanation needed.

"Then perhaps she should spend a quiet day at home, away from the sun," he suggested.

Melina scowled.

"Do you want us to be the boring grandparents and Valentina to prefer to spend her time with the other ones?"

Tanino didn't care about grandparental competition, but he cared about Melina, and he knew that she would be upset if he didn't take them to the beach.

So he dragged himself out of bed, resigned to a sticky day under the sun.

***

"Here we are," Tanino announced, pulling over on the seafront on the outskirts of Palermo.

"Where is the sand?" Melina asked.

"This is a pebble beach. So much better," Tanino replied. "No sand getting in between your toes and in your clothes."

"Can we still build sandcastles?" Valentina asked hopefully.

"I'm sorry, but that's not possible," Melina replied, scowling at Tanino.

Valentina looked crestfallen.

"But we can look for treasures," Melina suggested instead.

"What treasures?"

"Emeralds, rubies…"

"Oh yes, let's do that!" Valentina's eyes sparkled.

While Tanino unloaded the car, Melina and Valentina sat on the water's edge and searched.

They found black pebbles as shiny as liquorice, green pebbles that looked like jade, marbled pink pebbles and sea glass "emeralds".

"Wow, they're beautiful!" Valentina cried.

Maybe going to a pebble beach hadn't been such a disaster.

But then Valentina went on.

"Yesterday we built a sandcastle with a moat and a bridge. Then Nonno Stefano sat down on the beach and we covered his legs with sand until we couldn't see them anymore and he pretended he was trapped. But Nonna Alida called for lunch and he shook the sand off and got up. Nonno Stefano is very funny."

Melina glanced at Tanino, snoozing on his deckchair under his hat. He couldn't be any less entertaining if he tried.

"Can I take this pebble home?" Valentina asked.

"No, darling. The beach would become empty if everyone took home a pebble that big," Melina explained.

"But smaller ones I can?"

"A few, yes."

The hunt for the smallest pebbles was on. Eventually Valentina chose three to take home.

"Can you keep them safe for me?"

Melina had to put on her glasses to see the tiny orange quartz, the teeny green sea glass and the teensy white marble on Valentina's palm.

"Yes, sweetie."

"You won't lose them, will you?" Valentina asked.

"Of course not," Melina said confidently.

"Can we swim now?"

Melina didn't swim. Her contact with the sea was usually limited to a dip to cool down on a scorching mid-August day. But today was only June and it wasn't a scorching day.

"I'm very happy sitting here watching you. Nonno Tanino might swim with you," Melina suggested.

Tanino lifted the hat off his face and blinked.

"I left my swimming clothes at home," he said.

Melina suspected it hadn't been by accident.

"Why don't you swim on your own while we watch you from the shore?" she suggested to Valentina.

The girl's face fell.

"It's not fun swimming on my own. When I go to the beach with my other nonni, I swim with Gabriele, Emanuela and Monica."

A dagger went through Melina's heart. The other grandparents could provide cousins for Valentina to play with. She and Tanino could not.

"I'll come in the water with you," Melina

conceded.

The June sea was cold and Melina would much rather have been stretched on the deckchair next to Tanino's.

"Look at all the fish swimming round our legs!" Valentina cried, staring at the transparent water.

Melina would rather not know anything was swimming around her legs.

"Watch me!"

Valentina's somersault splashed those few remaining inches of skin Melina had managed to keep dry. She shivered.

"Now watch how long I can swim underwater!"

Valentina disappeared underwater for longer than Melina would have liked. When she re-emerged and took a big gulp of air, Melina took one too.

"Gabriele can stay underwater a lot longer," Valentina said, and went on to tell Melina about all the games she had played with her cousins.

Melina tried not to let her jealousy show. She and Tanino could never compete with the other nonni.

"Would you like to see me swim like a mermaid?" Valentina asked.

"I would," Melina said.

"I need to hold on to your hands," Valentina said.

Melina stretched out her hands and a horrible realization went through her mind. She shouldn't have two free hands! Where were the pebbles Valentina had given to her?

***

Valentina slept all the way home.

"She's exhausted. We've tired her out. I think she's enjoyed the trip a lot," Tanino said smugly.

Melina didn't comment. If Valentina hadn't already been disappointed by the lack of sand and the absence of cousins, she would be disappointed when she asked for her pebbles back.

Her other nonna would never have lost them.

***

Melina prodded her granddaughter gently.

"We're home."

Valentina opened her eyes slowly. As she recognised Melina's face and the car, she smiled.

"Can I have my pebbles?"

Melina's heart sank. This was the moment she had dreaded. There was nothing she could do but own up to her failure.

"I'm sorry, sweetheart. I've lost them."

A sad dimple formed on Valentina's chin.

"Can you search better?"

"I'm sure I dropped them in the sea," Melina explained, feeling smaller than the pebbles she had lost.

To her surprise, Valentina squeezed her in a hug.

"Don't be sad, Nonna. I lose things all the time. It's okay."

"Thank you," Melina replied, feeling better.

Valentina's mum, Rosanna, was already home, and as soon as she opened the door, Valentina started gushing about their trip.

"Nonna and I found treasures in the pebbles, we did roly-polies in the sea, we swam like mermaids…"

She didn't mention the lack of sand, the absence of cousins, nor the lost pebbles. In fact, in her retelling, her day out with Melina and Tanino sounded like a visit to the Garden of Eden. Melina wondered if perhaps Valentina's tale of her trip to the beach with the other nonni had been similarly edited.

"Thank you for taking her to the beach. It sounds like she's had a wonderful day," Rosanna said to Melina and Tanino after she sent Valentina for her shower.

"We try our best," Tanino said.

"Even if we'll never be able to compete with

her other nonni, who can offer the company of cousins," Melina added.

"You can offer something just as important: individual attention," Rosanna told them. "The other nonni have to share their attention. Sometimes she gets a little overwrought and tired after spending a day with them. You and Dad give her peace, quiet and one-on-one attention."

Melina felt lighter. Each set of grandparents had different things to offer.

"I thought that it might be nice to alternate the days she spends with you and with them, so one week you'd have her for two days, the next week you'd have her for three. How does that sound?" Rosanna continued.

"That sounds perfect!"

***

Melina always washed her swimsuits rigorously by hand.

She was just rinsing it in the bathroom sink when something shiny in the bottom of the basin caught her attention.

She put on her glasses. There they were. One tiny orange quartz, one teeny green sea glass and one teensy white pebble.

She pulled them out of the water, dried them carefully and rushed to fetch an empty jewellery box in which to store them safely. She couldn't wait to tell Valentina!

She imagined mounting the pebbles into a ring or a bracelet with some metal wire with Valentina. A quiet, relaxing activity for the next time she spent the day with them.

3. BREAK THE ICE

Marianna reordered the ice cream trays in her display. She liked to arrange them by colour rather than flavour, but it didn't seem to make any difference to the customers.

Whichever way she arranged them, they still didn't come. She had sold only one ice cream today. It must be because she was new to Palermo.

Sometimes she wondered if she'd made a mistake moving here to be closer to her daughter. City folks didn't seem to grant their trust as easily as the people of the village she had come from.

Even if she was only a few hundred meters away from her daughter, she might as well have been in another continent. Between them there was a great big wall, strict visiting times and rules that didn't allow bringing ice cream to the inmates.

Sometimes she dreamed of being a bird and

flying over the wall. Just catching a glimpse of her daughter, knowing that she was all right and telling her that she loved her would have been enough.

She busied herself wiping the counter one more time. A boy who must have been about twelve shot out of the alley towards her kiosk and crouched in the shade behind it.

A few seconds later, a group of boys ran out of the alley, looked around, then ran past. Maybe the boy wasn't hiding from the sun but from people.

As soon as she saw the group disappear off into another street, Marianna slid open her back window and whispered to the boy.

"They've gone."

He stepped out of the shadow. He had a fresh bruise on his cheekbone.

"I'd like an ice cream but I have no money."

"Before an ice cream, you need ice for that bruise."

Marianna wrapped a couple of ice cubes in a clean cloth and handed it to him.

Instead of putting the pack on his cheekbone, he unwrapped the ice and popped it in his mouth.

He looked at her with a cheeky grin.

"You're new," he remarked.

It was not a question.

"I'm not new. I'm fifty-one years old," she joked.

A smile kicked up at the corner of his lip and she noticed a spot of blood on his lips.

"Which flavour of ice cream would you like?"

"Chocolate."

She scooped some ice cream from the tray into a small cup and handed it to him.

"If you like it, tell all your friends," she said.

"I have no friends."

"I'm sorry."

"Don't be: you don't have any friends either."

He was perceptive.

"Well, we can still be sorry for each other."

"Or we could be friends." He blew his hair out of his eyes but it immediately flopped back down.

"That's a much better idea." She smiled. "I'm Marianna. And you?"

"I'm not." Slowly and luxuriously, he licked the ice cream, closed his eyes and smacked his lips together.

"This ice cream is de-li-cious!" he cried.

A grandmother and granddaughter, who were admiring the windows of the clothing shop opposite, turned to look.

A little later, they were asking for the same

ice cream that the boy had, one for each.

As soon as they had gone, Marianna turned to her new friend.

"Thanks for that. I think that you deserve a whole ice cream. What would you like?"

He asked for three different flavours in a brioche bun, the Sicilian way, with whipped cream and a biscuit on top. The works.

"You'll have to work a bit more for all this," she warned him.

"I sure will."

As soon as he got the ice cream, he started strutting down the street, singing between each lick.

"It's a treat; it's a dream—
it's Marianna's fresh ice cream!
Her chocolate is the best:
it's a cut above the rest.
Try it with coconut, berries or toffee,
or, if you like it, have it with coffee.
For good health, try hazelnut
which works wonders for your gut.
Lemon is excellent, so is pistachio
if you don't mind a green mustachio.
The most refreshing—take my hint—
is the strawberry with the mint.
Another favourite of this fella
is the lovely *stracciatella*.
And if you don't love her lush vanilla,

you're a madman or a gorilla!"

Marianna was speechless. Not only had the boy memorised her entire menu and rhymed it, but he had a great singing voice too!

Customers flocked to her kiosk, bought ice cream and congratulated her for his talent, as if she was related to him.

"You're a good singer," she told him at the end.

"I know. My dad told me and he knows about music."

"Your father is a singer?"

"He sells CDs in the streets with his cart."

As if telling her about his dad had unlocked another level of friendship, he continued.

"I'm Giuseppe. I have to go now. See you tomorrow."

With that, he sauntered off and disappeared back into the alley.

Marianna felt a lightness in her chest that she hadn't experienced in a long time, and she was already looking forward to seeing him again tomorrow. She had made her first friend in Palermo.

***

Giuseppe wasn't running when he emerged from the alley this time.

His hair was combed back and gelled, and his clothes, although still tatty and old, had the fold lines of garments freshly taken out of a drawer. Had he dressed up?

"Which ice cream would you like?" she asked him.

"I'm not eating while I'm working," he stated, slightly scandalised.

If he wasn't thinking of repeating yesterday's performance while eating her ice cream, how was he thinking of helping her?

"What kind of work are you offering to do?"

"The same as you. If you don't trust me with the money, you can take the payments."

Marianna smiled. She loved his straight, open ways.

"You can take the money. I trust you," she said.

"Do you always trust people so quickly?" He sounded curious and surprised, not mocking.

"Where I come from, we do," she explained.

Business that day was booming, especially when the afternoon-shift schoolchildren came out. People recognised Giuseppe and greeted him.

"How do you know so many people?" Marianna asked him.

"They're customers of Grandpa's cobbler shop. I told them I'd put extra ice cream on especially for them."

"But you didn't ask me first!"

"How will they know if I'm giving them more ice cream or just the same that you would have?" He winked.

Marianna was speechless. Giuseppe was a bottomless pit of surprises.

That day, for the first time, she made a profit.

Giuseppe returned the next day and every day after. If there were enough customers, he helped in the kiosk. Otherwise, he went off into the streets, singing at the top of his voice.

One day, a group of boys timidly approached the kiosk, keeping their distance. Marianna immediately senses Giuseppe's tension. Were they the ones who were pursuing him the day she first met him?

"We don't have to serve them if we don't want to," she whispered to him.

"I don't mind them. They can't hurt me now. I have a friend," he whispered back.

Marianna guessed that he meant emotional hurt. Maybe the wounds she hadn't seen had been worse than the bruised cheek and bloody lip.

Giuseppe raised his voice. "How can I help you?"

Sheepishly, the boys came forward and politely asked him for three ice cream cones.

Giuseppe served them and they paid him,

thanked him and said goodbye.

Marianna felt that this was the boys' way to ask and give forgiveness.

***

"Don't come tomorrow. I'm closing the kiosk early," Marianna warned Giuseppe on Friday night.

He looked disappointed.

"Why? There are always lots of customers on a Saturday afternoon."

"I'm going to visit my daughter."

It was the third Saturday of the month and it was visiting day at the prison. Marianna couldn't wait and she wouldn't sleep tonight.

"Can't you see her later, after closing?"

She could simply have answered "no". Giuseppe would have understood that she didn't want to say anything more.

Back in her village, being the mother of a convict had carried stigma and shame.

Here in the city, where nobody knew her story, she could wipe the slate clean and start anew.

But it felt wrong to keep such a big a secret from her new friend. Her daughter in prison was the reason she was here, the object of her prayers, her constant thought, and she longed to have someone to talk about her with.

"I can only visit her during the prison's

visiting times."

Giuseppe looked thoughtful but not shocked.

"Okay, you can visit her," he said, as if Marianna somehow belonged to him and he was granting her permission.

She smiled.

"How long ago did you see her last?" he asked.

"Too long. I often envy the birds because they can fly over that wall and sing for the people inside."

Giuseppe's eyes flashed as if he'd just had an idea.

"Then, when you see her tomorrow, tell her to look out for a surprise to come."

***

Giuseppe's father, Salvatore, must have been a teenager when Giuseppe was born because he looked like he was only in his early twenties.

He had the same cheeky smile and the same floppy hair that he occasionally blew out of his eyes. He was trying to explain to Marianna how the microphone worked but she was too excited to focus.

"You're not listening, are you?" he asked her.

He sounded just like his son.

"No. I'm too excited," she admitted. "Just

tell me what to do when we get there."

He rolled his eyes and smiled. The cart had been emptied of all the CDs. All that was left were the enormous speakers and the microphone.

He lifted the handles and pushed it as if it weighed no more than an empty wheelbarrow. Marianna and Giuseppe followed.

When they got close enough to the prison's walls, but not so close as to annoy the guards, Salvatore put on the music.

It was the lullaby that Marianna used to sing to her daughter when she was little.

Marianna didn't have a good singing voice, so Giuseppe took the microphone and started singing the verses.

The beautiful notes soared over the walls, echoing against the distant Monte Pellegrino. There was no way that anyone inside the prison wouldn't hear it.

At the end, Salvatore passed the microphone to Marianna. She had tears in her eyes and a heart full of longing and love.

"Goodnight, sweetheart. I love you," she said into the microphone.

Her daughter would know that it was her, and everyone else in the prison would feel the love too.

A mixture of clapping, rattling and cheering

rose from the prison, and Marianna knew that among them was her daughter's heartfelt smile.

4. BEST SERVED COLD

Few people irritated Rosalia as much as her neighbour in the flat above. That woman had the habit of washing her balcony with bucketfuls of water, sending all the muck down onto Rosalia's balcony and her laundry hung out to dry.

When she wasn't recreating the Niagara Falls, she was beating carpets, shaking dusters, sweeping leaves off, as if no one lived below her.

Rosalia had complained many times, but her neighbour kept doing it. Rosalia felt that the proverb, "*goccia a goccia scava la roccia*", "drop by drop digs the rock", had been invented for her. She was the rock being dug out. And, one day, she cracked.

***

The force of gravity played against her, but Rosalia didn't give up. Water flowed down but hot air went up.

Like many others in Palermo, Rosalia used her balcony as an overflow kitchen and laundry. There she kept her washing machine, an emergency water butt and a little gas stove for especially messy cooking. She used it for frying and cooking fish and anything with an unpleasant smell.

That day, Rosalia waited for her neighbour to do her weekly whites wash. As soon as the bedsheets were hanging off her washing line, Rosalia turned on her stove and filled it with oil.

She got a batch of sardines out of the freezer and dropped them in. Oh, how they hopped and crackled in the oil! And the smell—oh, the smell! Not an aroma you'd like to find on your clean laundry. Rosalia grinned with satisfaction.

***

The first time, Carmela gave her neighbour the benefit of the doubt. It had happened at lunchtime, so Rosalia could have genuinely needed to do a fish fry-up. But the second time Rosalia smoked her laundry, it was nine o' clock in the morning.

The two women became locked in such a cycle of retaliation that Carmela's husband was convinced that his wife had a cleaning mania, and Rosalia's suspected that his wife had a thing for the fishmonger.

But on one hot August afternoon, all could have turned to tragedy. Because, while she was smoking Carmela's laundry, Rosalia's doorbell rang.

It was her next-door neighbour—a woman Rosalia liked very much—and she had big news: her daughter was getting married.

As they talked about wedding dresses and flowers, Rosalia completely forgot her fish on the stove. While the women chatted, the sardines danced in the oil until they turned charcoal black.

At that point, the oil boiled over and met up with the fire. It was an instant connection, a spark of understanding, love at first sight. Flames whooshed up from the pan, singeing the edges of the fly curtain, ready to spill over.

The fire was just about to leap onto the fly curtain, which the littlest breath of wind could have pushed into the kitchen, setting the plastic tablecloth on fire. The seats of the chairs would have readily received the flames and passed them on to the kitchen cupboards, where flour, pasta and crackers would have burst into flames. What could have happened next doesn't bear thinking about.

***

The fishy smell was so powerful that Carmela sniffed it from the other side of the kitchen.

She had just put her washing out on the lines and was expecting the smoking treatment, but this time her neighbour had gone over the top. This smelled of burning! Did Rosalia hate her so much that she was willing to burn her own lunch just to upset her?

Carmela grabbed her bucket, filled it with water and splashed it over her balcony's floor, then another bucket, and some more. In the end, she didn't even pretend to wash the floor and just poured the water over the edge. If her water put out Rosalia's stove, all the better. That woman deserved it.

***

"Good Heavens!" Rosalia jumped when the smell of burnt fish reached her nose.

She left her next-door neighbour standing at her door and ran back in and out to her balcony.

Where her fish had been was now drenched charcoal. The blackened frying pan told her that fire hadn't been just under it.

There was water everywhere, pooling in puddles, dripping from the railings and from the edges of the balcony above.

There had been a pan fire and her neighbour had put it out, saving her flat, her possessions and maybe even her life!

Tears brimmed in her eyes. She ran out of

her flat, past her other neighbour who was asking her lots of worried questions, and rushed up the stairs, panting with the effort.

***

At the sound of the doorbell, Carmela's heart stopped. It had to be Rosalia.

Until then, all their quarrels had happened from the safety of their balconies. If Rosalia had gone as far as climbing the stairs and ringing her doorbell, she must be furious.

Carmela decided to ignore the door.

But the bell rang again, urgently. Clearly Rosalia was going to drive her crazy with that bell.

Carmela padded silently to her front door and put her eye to the peephole. Oh no, Rosalia was mad at her: panting, red in the face, eyes shiny with tears. No way could she face her in that state. She closed the peephole and retreated to the furthest room in the flat.

***

"You are the talk of the building, my darling," Carmela's husband announced when he got home from work.

Carmela's blood ran cold. Rosalia had told everyone.

"I'm sorry, things got out of control, I didn't mean to upset her that much—"

"The pan fire you put out could have spread

to the whole flat," her husband carried on, "and who knows where else? Rosalia is praising you to the stars."

It took Carmela a few seconds to process the information. So the pan had actually been on fire, and Rosalia wasn't mad at her.

"Silly me, I thought that the two of you didn't get on!" Her husband chuckled.

Carmela grinned. Rosalia was praising her. Wow. "Oh no, we have always liked each other."

Just then, the doorbell rang. Carmela jumped from her chair.

***

Carmela opened the door and Rosalia pulled her into a teary hug.

"I'm so sorry. I was frying the fish on purpose to make your laundry smell, while you have been so kind to me!" Rosalia confessed, full of regret.

Carmela hugged Rosalia back.

"Don't mention it, it's all forgotten. We shall never talk about it again," Carmela said. She meant it.

She had no intention of confessing that she had put the fire out by accident. It wouldn't be helpful to their new friendship. And, from now on, she would never do anything to damage their relationship.

5. SAND, SEA & TAMBURELLO

Rosa imagined the sand creeping up the tubular metal legs of her folding chair. She hated going to the beach when she couldn't swim. The sticky sand and the searing sun were fun only if you could find respite in the cool water.

But it was her time of the month and even just wearing her swimming suit would be awkward, in the circumstances. So there she was, sitting on a folding chair under her family's old beach umbrella, wearing comfortable shorts which suggested her predicament to every passer-by.

Everyone except her seven-year-old brother.

"Why isn't Rosa swimming?" Giovannino asked their mother after two minutes.

He did that every time.

"Women's business," Mum replied, like she did every time.

Rosa hid behind her magazine. She usually

went straight to the photo story and read until the glare of the sun made her eyes hurt, but today she started with the main story: Ringo Starr was having a tonsillectomy. She hoped that British surgeons knew their stuff because she would never entrust her favourite Beatle's throat to some of the Sicilian ones.

She thought about lunch and the tray of pasta bake she could look forward to. It had seemed like a terrific idea in the morning, when she'd helped Mum cook it, but now it felt way too heavy and unrefreshing for a day in the sun, without swimming in the sea.

She took a swig from her metal water bottle. Even the water had turned to hot soup. If only Mum and Dad had let her stay at home.

"If we were going for a few hours, yes. But not for the entire day," Mum objected when Rosa asked.

Rosa thought that she could have said the same about coming to the beach.

"Will you play *tamburello* with me?" Giovannino thrust the tambourine-shaped racket on Rosa's lap.

"No, thanks."

"Why?"

"I don't want to get sweaty."

"If you get sweaty, jump into the sea."

"I can't."

"Why?"

Rosa rolled her eyes. "Just leave me alone."

Giovannino tottered off and she followed him with her gaze. He asked Dad if he would play, but Dad shook his head and stretched himself on his towel.

Mum had already disappeared in the water, leaving a trail of rubber flowers which had broken free from her swimming cap.

Rosa sighed. Lucky people. The water sparkled and quivered in its aquamarine beauty, stretching to the horizon where seagulls and sailing boats mingled their snow-white wings. The transparent water looked good enough to drink.

"Will you play with me?" Giovannino's voice rang from a distance.

Who could he be asking now? Rosa turned to look. Her brother was harassing a stranger— a boy about her own age—thrusting the tamburello racket at him. Mum was in the water and Dad was asleep on the sand. It was Rosa's duty to shout to Giovannino to leave the stranger in peace.

Rosa sprang to her feet, filled her lungs to bellow, but her breath stuck in her throat. The stranger was looking at her.

He wasn't handsome in a fashionable way, but there was something about his warm smile and his demeanour that attracted her. For one thing, he was now looking at her little brother with interest rather than irritation.

"Sure," he said, taking the racket from Giovannino.

The boy led Giovannino to a patch of beach without towels or umbrellas and they started playing. Rosa turned her chair so that she could keep an eye on them and sat down.

The other boy started off with some very good throws but then adjusted his game to suit Giovannino's limited skills. Each time Giovannino didn't manage to catch the ball, they took it in turns to retrieve it. Except when the ball landed on somebody's beach towel or sandcastle—then the boy always went to retrieve it, sparing Giovannino the embarrassment.

After a good half an hour, Giovannino began to look droopy and, a little later, he dropped his racket in the middle of the game and sat on the sand while the ball flew over his head.

"I'm tired," he said.

Typical of her brother.

The other boy kindly ran after the ball. Giovannino then got up and said something to his companion, who started following him.

Rosa's heart went into overdrive as she saw

them coming towards her. She dusted the sand off her legs and wiped the sweat off her face with the edge of a sandy towel.

"This is my sister," Giovannino said, pointing unceremoniously to her. "She can't swim today: she's doing women's business," he declared solemnly.

Rosa wished the sand would swallow her. Her cheeks whooshed on fire. The stranger pinned his eyes on his feet and, even under his golden suntan, she could see him blush pink.

"But my friend and I can swim, can't we, Rosa?" Giovannino asked her.

"Yes, you can," she muttered with the little voice she could summon.

She watched them from under the brim of her sunhat as the two of them walked away together, the chubby little boy clinging onto the arm of the tall, sinewy boy with narrow hips and handsome straight shoulders. And Rosa wished she was the one holding the handsome lad's hand.

***

"You've made a new friend today," Rosa commented with pretend nonchalance to Giovannino.

Now that they were in the car on the way home, there was no way he could embarrass her again with the stranger.

"Yes. He's very nice," Giovannino replied.

"What's his name?" she asked casually.

"I don't know."

"What have you been talking about for all that time?"

"You."

Rosa's breath caught in her throat, just as Dad pulled the choke to start the Fiat 500's engine.

"W-what did you say about me?"

"I told him that you play tamburello very well and you're fun when you don't have women's business. I told him that sisters are nice and he should get one too."

The Fiat's engine shuddered to life.

"What did he say about getting a sister too?" Rosa asked, smiling.

"Nothing. He wanted to know more about you."

The car leapt forward and so did Rosa's heart.

***

"You were ever so red in the face yesterday at the beach," Mum said to Rosa as they wrapped today's pasta bake tray in a tea towel.

Rosa wondered if her mum was referring to the sun's heat or her embarrassment.

"If you don't feel like coming to the beach and getting hot again today, you can stay home.

I've asked Maria next door to keep an ear open for you, if you need anything."

Rosa was reassured that her mum's comment was just about the heat.

"No, thanks. I want to come with you," Rosa replied without hesitation, then hastily added, "I've promised Giovannino a game of tamburello."

Mum stilled and looked into her eyes.

"I'm very happy that you want to come with us. But remember: beach romances last as long as the tide."

Rosa's cheeks burned and she looked away. Yes, her mother had noticed everything.

***

Pino was glad to have agreed to play with the little boy, Giovannino, even if it meant missing out on seeing his friends at the pier that day. The boy was sweet and his sister sounded even sweeter.

It was touching how much he loved her. From what he had told him about her, she sounded like a really nice girl and, when Giovannino had suggested that he get a sister too, Pino had almost said, "I'll happily share yours!"

That morning, when Giovannino's family arrived at the beach, Pino made himself busy fixing his family's crooked beach umbrella. He didn't want them to think that he had been scanning the beach searching for them for the past hour, which was exactly what he'd been doing.

"Hello! I'm ready to play and Rosa is going to play with us too!" Giovannino shouted, running towards him.

Pino turned around and his heart skipped a beat. There she was, racket in one hand, the other hand holding her arm shyly. She looked beautiful.

"That's great," he said, smiling at her.

As they started the game, Pino reminded himself to resist the temptation to show off but keep it easy for Giovannino so that he wouldn't get bored and go away, taking Rosa with him.

Pino couldn't have played any harder anyway, distracted as he was by Rosa's presence. She was very good at tamburello and it was clear that she, too, was making an effort to keep the game slow for Giovannino.

Each time he received the ball from Rosa's racket, Pino felt a frisson of excitement as if he was touching Rosa's hand.

After a little while, Giovannino dropped his racket and sat down on the sand. Pino already knew that this meant that the game was over.

"I'm hot. I want to swim," Giovannino announced.

Pino glanced at Rosa and saw his disappointment reflected in her face too. She wasn't wearing a swimming suit today either.

"How about drinking some water? It'll make you feel better, then you can play tamburello a little more," she suggested to her brother.

Sweat beaded her upper lip and forehead. She must be thirsty too, but instead of suggesting she got a drink too, she told her brother, "While you get your drink, we'll keep the ball in the air without letting it drop. I bet that we can."

"No, you can't!" her brother protested.

"Yes, we can, and we'll show you."

Rosa smiled at Pino and his heart floated. They were a team together.

While Giovannino sat under his family's umbrella, sipping water as if it was wine and shouting, "I'm still drinking!", Pino and Rosa carried on playing together, diving, leaping, running for the ball, as light as birds on the wings of infatuation.

But eventually Giovannino returned and insisted that he wanted to swim.

"You two go. I'll take a rest under the umbrella," Rosa said.

Reluctantly, Pino left her behind and accompanied Giovannino in the water. Never mind, he told himself: the season had only just started and there would be more chances to be with Rosa.

In fact, they met again the following day and the one after. Games of tamburello were followed by swims and water games. Giovannino always demanded to dive off Pino's shoulders into the water. Rosa always seemed to know when Pino's shoulders were getting sore, and distracted her brother with other games.

By now she could swim again, and she swished in the water like a mermaid, with her olive skin glittering in the sun and her long hair trailing behind her. Pino realised that they were still young, but he knew that, one day, he would ask her to be his wife.

One day, when Giovannino had swum off, leaving them alone, Rosa said, "Giovannino always calls you 'my friend' so I don't know your name yet."

"Giuseppe, but everyone calls me Pino. Actually, my mum calls me Spino, *thorn*, when I'm being a thorn in the flesh," he said with a chuckle. Then, turning serious, he added, "You are Rosa, *rose*, and the saying goes that there's no rose without a thorn."

Her cheeks instantly turned pink like rose petals, and she averted her gaze.

Pino instantly regretted the words that had

tumbled out of his mouth. He had gone too far and embarrassed her. Luckily, just then, Giovannino called from the pontoon, "Come and join me!"

For the rest of that day, there was a certain awkwardness between them. If it hadn't been for Giovannino, Rosa would have probably retreated under the family's umbrella.

The following day, when the sun was already high but there was still no sign of Giovannino and Rosa's family, Pino concluded that they weren't coming anymore because of what he'd said. What a stupid idiot he'd been, and how presumptuous to say that she couldn't exist without him! He should have said "there's no thorn without a rose", even if that wasn't scientifically true.

Just as he was about to head off to the pier to join his friends, he recognised a small voice shouting, "We're here!"

It was Giovannino with Rosa and their parents. Suddenly the sea sparkled more, the sand felt softer and the world an altogether better place.

Giovannino ran up to him.

"Our car broke down! We had to walk!"

***

Rosa's heart swelled in her chest when she saw Pino on the beach, looking like he had been waiting for them.

She couldn't forget the words he had told her. She had thought about them all night.

"My dad has jump leads and a tow rope in the car. Would you like me to ask him to help you?" Pino offered their Dad.

"Yes, please."

Signor Liotta seemed more than happy to help and offered to drive Rosa's dad back to their car in his Alfa Romeo Giulia.

"We want to come too!" Giovannino shouted, interpreting Rosa's wishes too.

Their desire was granted. As the two dads rode in the front of the Giulia, their children travelled in the back, with Giovannino sitting between Rosa and Pino.

Their Fiat 500 was still where they'd left it. Pino helped his dad with the jumpstart leads and Rosa admired his skills and knowledge. In a short time, the car was fixed and was running again.

"Get in the car, kids," Dad said.

"Can I have another ride in the Giulia?" Giovannino pined.

"By all means, if your father agrees," Signor Liotta replied, flattered.

"Only if your sister comes with you," Dad replied.

"Sure," Rosa answered readily.

So off they went, Giovannino in the place of honour on the front next to Signor Liotta, while Rosa and Pino sat in the back, sliding closer together at every corner of the road.

When they got back to the beach, the mothers were chatting together chummily.

"They are a nice family," her mother whispered in Rosa's ear.

When it was time to leave, Mum and Dad invited the Liottas to dinner at their home as a thank you for their help with the car. They readily agreed.

**

Many years later

"Can you play tamburello with me?" Nino asked Pino.

"I never say no to a game of tamburello," Pino replied, sending Rosa a meaningful glance. "Neither does your grandma."

"Grandma, play with us!" Nino piped.

"I'm not as good as I was when I was fourteen," Rosa admitted.

"Your grandmother was a great player. But she didn't show off: instead, she played slowly to make sure that her brother didn't get bored," Pino said with a smile.

"Is that the great-uncle I'm named after?" the boy asked, "Nino" being a shortened version of Giovannino.

"Yes."

Rosa smiled dreamily, thinking of her little brother, who had brought her and Pino together. He was no longer with them but his memory lived on in their grandchild, in their marriage, and in the game of tamburello.

6. SAFE AS HOUSES

Tanino inspected his beloved mulberry tree. There were plenty of ripening fruits but, thankfully, no silkworms to devour the leaves.

When he was younger, he'd heard that there had been a lot of silkworm farms in Sicily before the war, and mulberry tree orchards stretched across that area. But not now. His mulberry tree was all for him, not for sharing with any worms, and if he was lucky, tonight Melina would make her delicious mulberry sorbet with the fruits he was harvesting.

This was one of the pleasures of spending time at a summer house in the countryside.

Technically, the house and the garden belonged to his friend, Giacomo, but he had granted Tanino use of the place this year in exchange for maintenance of the house and care of the garden and orchard.

So, even though Tanino lived in a flat for most of the year, he could still spend time immersed in nature at weekends and during the warmer season and enjoy home-grown produce.

His dog, Bello, loved it too, Tanino thought, watching him chase a butterfly.

"Hello, Tanino, how are you?" his next-door neighbour called over the drystone wall.

"Very well, thanks, and you?"

The other man rolled his eyes and sighed.

"I've had a break-in." He gestured to his house, nestled in his olive grove.

"I didn't think there would be burglars up here on these mountains."

Tanino couldn't imagine any burglar in his right mind driving up the miles of dirt track that led to their little houses.

He looked around at the rolling hills. Citrus orchards and prickly pear cactuses were in bloom. A burglary felt as out of place as it would in the Garden of Eden.

"They weren't burglars: they didn't take anything. All they did was eat our food and sleep in our beds."

Tanino remembered a story he had read to his granddaughter about a blonde, curly-haired girl who had done just the same to a family of bears.

"Why?"

"I reckon that they were shepherds looking

for shelter. We found sheep droppings everywhere! I'm telling you so that you can take precautions. It could be your house next."

"I always lock up with double rounds," Tanino said.

"That's not enough. I'm getting a guard dog," the man said.

Tanino looked down at Bello who was wagging his tail at a lizard.

"I already have one."

His neighbour smiled pitifully.

"I meant a proper guard dog. Tanino, if you think that I'm overreacting because the intruders didn't steal anything, you're wrong. This break-in has cost me a lot of money. My wife has insisted on replacing everything in the house: mattresses, towels, bedlinen—you name it!"

Tanino hadn't thought about that. Melina would react in the same way. He shuddered. She might even call the pest control people.

***

"What were you talking about with the neighbour?" Melina asked her husband.

"They've had a break-in but nothing was stolen. He thinks that they were shepherds looking for shelter," Tanino said.

He looked intently at her, as if to gauge her reaction.

"Poor shepherds, I don't blame them. There were terrible gales last winter," Melina said.

"You don't blame them for breaking into people's homes?"

"There's no such thing as private property when lives are at risk. The weather can be dangerous up on the mountains. I watched a documentary on TV about the Alps. Did you know that there are mountain huts with beds, blankets, water and food, where anyone can take shelter for the night without paying a thing?"

"We're not in the Alps. We're in Sicily," Tanino said.

"Besides, this house doesn't actually belong to us."

"Giacomo has allowed us to use it as if it was."

"All the more reason to be generous to others. I'm sure Giacomo would agree. We could leave the door unlocked, with a message inviting people to go in if the weather is bad..."

"Nobody has ever done that."

"...and leave some food..."

"They'd think it was a trick. Poisoned."

"...and hay for the animals," Melina said. Tanino sighed.

"I'm going to buy a new padlock."

***

"It's the best padlock on the market," the owner of the hardware shop told Tanino.

It was pricey, but surely less expensive than replacing all the mattresses, bedding and towels in the house, and explaining to Giacomo that his house had been broken into on Tanino's watch.

"I'll take it."

The shopkeeper leant over the counter and lowered his voice.

"If you are really concerned about security, a padlock alone won't do. You need a light on a sensor."

He rummaged behind the counter and pulled out a box with the picture of a man in a balaclava trying to force open a door.

"The next step is, of course, CCTV. If it's prominent enough, it'll work as a deterrent. If not, it'll still help identify the culprits."

Tanino checked the price tag and swallowed. It had to be close to the cost of replacing all soft furnishings in the house. Even though he'd run his plan past his friend, it wouldn't be fair to ask Giacomo to share the cost, considering how rarely he stayed at the house.

The shopkeeper continued.

"If you are serious about the security of your home, you have to spend the money. Don't they say that a man's home is his castle? Well,

I say it's his fortress."

Then he pulled out another box.

"A burglar alarm is an essential for security, and this one is special. As well as the usual sirens, this one gives you the option to record your own sounds. For example, you could record your dog's bark!"

The man glanced down at Bello and frowned slightly.

"Or maybe you could record yourself saying things like, 'The police are on their way'. But if you choose one of the sirens, the sound is so unbearable that any intruder will flee."

It was going to be expensive, but no price was too high for peace of mind.

"I'll have everything," Tanino said.

He was just leaving when the shopkeeper added, "Remember, a padlock is only as good as the door."

Tanino's peace of mind instantly fizzled away.

He dropped off his shopping at home, phoned Giacomo, collected his chequebook and set off again.

***

Three months later, four men were installing a new impregnable door, when one of them looked at the ground floor windows and shook his head.

"There's no point having an armoured door if the burglars can come in through the windows," he said.

Tanino felt like crying.

That very day, he contacted a company that put bars on windows. They came the following week and installed metal bars on every window.

With its armoured door, CCTV, burglar alarm and metal bars, Giacomo's summer house now looked like a fortress.

Tanino could finally close it for the winter and return to his flat, where he would wait for spring with perfect peace of mind.

***

"Why are you going so early? It's not even March yet," Melina asked her husband when he announced that he was going to open the summer house.

"I want to check on the plants," he said.

"I'll go with you."

But when they got there, Tanino didn't rush to his beloved mulberry tree, or to his apple trees or to his vines. Instead, he rushed to the house.

A moment later, he returned to the car, looking ashen.

"What's wrong?" Melina asked, but she needn't have.

Just looking at the house would have given

her the answer.

"Goodness! Why has Giacomo changed the door and put those ugly bars on the windows?"

"I did it. I had them installed before the winter."

Tanino must have had the work done just when she had stopped coming because it was too cold, so she had never seen them. If it had been Tanino's own doing, then why was he upset?

"What's the problem, then?"

He looked sheepishly at her.

"When I closed up for the winter, I forgot to lock the door."

***

Tanino couldn't believe he had done something so stupid.

What was the point of burglar-proofing the house if he didn't bother locking the door? Anyone could have walked in. Luckily, nobody had.

Tanino should be feeling grateful and pleased about it. Instead, he felt rejected. The shepherds had gone to the trouble of breaking into his neighbour's house, but they hadn't deigned to visit his house, even when the door was open.

Maybe the fortified look of the house had discouraged passing shepherds from even trying. He had made his house unwelcoming. He felt a little like the Scrooge character of the classic story, and sadness swept over him.

Meanwhile, Melina was inspecting the house.

"I'm not sure I like the bars on the windows. What's the point of a holiday home if it feels like a prison?"

She was right.

"I'm sure we can have them removed," he said.

He stepped into the house and a loud, "Get out or I'll call the police!" boomed out of a speaker above his head.

He jumped out of his skin. It was his own recorded voice. At least he hadn't forgotten to set the burglar alarm.

***

The apple trees blossomed, the mulberries ripened and the vines produced their grapes. Then it came time to lock up for winter again.

It was a blustery and cold day, and Melina remembered that, a while ago, Tanino had told her about some shepherds who had broken into their neighbour's house to find shelter. Poor things.

"Do you think Giacomo would mind if we left the garage open for passing shepherds caught out in the weather?" she asked Tanino gingerly.

He had removed the bars from the windows and had returned the armoured door to the shop, but wouldn't it be better if the shepherds didn't have to break in to find shelter?

"Yes, dear. We could also leave some food, water and hay for the animals," he said.

Melina smiled. That was her man!

***

Spring came again and Tanino and Melina returned to the house.

The first thing they inspected wasn't the mulberry tree, nor the vines or even the house. Instead, they went straight to the garage.

On the little table where they had left food for the shepherds, there was now a wheel of pecorino cheese, with a message: *Thank you.*

7. NOT SO LOUD

Alfonso stepped out of the car and took a lungful of fresh sea air. He had waited all year for this moment: the first day of his summer holidays.

A spray of purple bougainvillea cascaded over the fence that separated his garden from his neighbour's, and the oleander's pink blossom filled the air with its sweet scent. The hibiscus in bloom buzzed with bees. This was the Sicilian summer at his best.

"Do you know who has bought the house next door?" his wife, Sandra asked. "It looks like the new owners have moved in."

She pointed to the sensible car parked on the neighbouring drive.

"No idea, but they've done a good job on the drystone wall. And that rusty gate was in urgent need of replacement. I'm glad they got a new one," Alfonso said.

"I love those potted geraniums that they've

put on the steps. It gives the place a classy touch. I already like our new neighbours." Sandra smiled.

"Tomorrow we shall visit and introduce ourselves," Alfonso declared.

That evening, Alfonso and Sandra were admiring the sunset on their terrace when a skin-curling screech of a microphone making feedback with an amplifier broke the blissful silence.

"One, two, three, testing, testing," boomed a voice.

It came from their neighbour's house. A moment later, a karaoke machine pumped the air with the notes of the summer's chart hits. It was so loud that it kneaded Alfonso's stomach and pummelled his temples. Sandra stared back at him, wide-eyed.

"He must be testing the volume," she said hopefully.

Minutes passed, then hours, but the karaoke machine continued blasting music at the same volume.

To make matters worse, the neighbour bellowed the songs' lyrics out of tune and others joined in too. As the night went on, their voices grew hoarser but they didn't stop.

Alfonso and Sandra gave up their plans of a quiet evening out on their terrace and retreated inside, where they hunkered down with windows and doors closed.

***

That night, the karaoke went on until well after midnight, and the following morning neither Alfonso nor Sandra mentioned visiting their neighbours.

They sipped their morning coffee on their terrace, listening to the waves lapping at the shore and the distant rumble of the fishermen's boats returning to the harbour after a night's fishing.

"Maybe last night was just a housewarming party," Sandra said.

"I hope so."

Even the fish in the sea must have been disturbed.

But later that day, a crackle and a whistle heralded the beginning of another karaoke session. Alfonso and Sandra barricaded themselves indoors with windows shut despite the stifling heat. Was this how they would spend the rest of their summer holiday?

"Those geranium pots are quite garish, actually," Sandra said, looking at their neighbours' steps.

"And I don't like their new gate," Alfonso said.

When the karaoke finally stopped, a stunned

silence filled the bay like the quiet after the storm.

The following day, when the karaoke started again, Alfonso and Sandra were prepared with ear plugs. Unfortunately, the plugs didn't stop the bass notes pummelling their stomachs.

"This isn't working, is it?" Alfonso said that evening.

Sandra shook her head.

"Then we have no choice left but to report the neighbours to the police."

The next afternoon, as soon as the karaoke started, Alfonso rang the police.

"We're overstretched. We'll log it and look into it when we have time," they told him.

Alfonso realised that they never would.

"All this noise can't be good for the wildlife either," Sandra said.

They called the Society for the Protection of Seabirds, the Coastline Conservation Council and even the WWF, but they all said the karaoke problem was outside their remit.

Meanwhile, the karaoke tracks had moved from pop to rock. Would heavy metal be next?

Desperation sharpened Alfonso's mind. He picked up his toolbox and set off out of his gate.

***

Vittorio was halfway through The Rolling

Stone's *I Can't Get No Satisfaction*, when his karaoke machine stopped, his microphone died and the lights went off.

"Have we had a power cut?" his wife, Carolina, asked from the kitchen.

Their entire house was in darkness.

"I think it's just us," Vittorio said, looking out from their terrace at the rest of the bay, which was still all lit up.

He checked the house's fuse box but everything was in order. Maybe something had gone wrong during the change of ownership?

He called the electricity suppliers, who confirmed the account was in order.

"We'll send someone tomorrow morning," they told him.

No amount of begging from Vittorio achieved anything: they were not going to look into it before the morning. Vittorio had to resign himself to the fact that, for that night, there would be no karaoke, no light, no aircon.

"Our phones' batteries are almost down to zero," the kids said.

"And we haven't got torches or candles," Carolina said.

"Why don't we ask the neighbours?" their son suggested.

"Are they here?" Vittorio asked.

"There's a car on their drive and light in their

windows," their daughter said.

Vittorio had been so busy with his karaoke machine that he hadn't noticed anything around him.

"We should have gone and introduced ourselves. It would be rude to turn up just to ask for things."

"This is an emergency. We can introduce ourselves at the same time."

***

Peace and quiet, at last. Alfonso had never been more pleased to be a qualified electrician, because he had been able to cut off only his neighbour's power supply without affecting anyone else's.

He sneaked back into the house, put away his toolbox and joined his wife on the terrace.

The sea glittered with moonlight and a gentle breeze carried the scent of jasmine, oleander and geranium. It was pure bliss.

"I truly hope that Karaoke Man doesn't start again," Sandra said.

"I'm sure that he won't tonight." Alfonso smiled.

"Hello? Is anyone in?" someone called from their gate.

Alfonso recognised the voice immediately. He froze. Had Karaoke Man realised that he was responsible for the power cut?

"Are you expecting anyone?" Sandra asked.

"No," Alfonso lied. A shiver ran down his back.

"We're your new neighbours," Karaoke Man called from the gate.

We? Alfonso peered at their gate and quivered. Karaoke Man had brought reinforcements. Things were going to get nasty.

"Aren't we going to answer?" Sandra asked.

"I guess we have no choice."

As they plodded down the stairs, Alfonso prepared himself for the inevitable confrontation.

But as soon as he got to the gate, even in the pale light of the moon, Alfonso could see that the neighbours weren't the monsters he had imagined. They were even smiling.

"Sorry we haven't come round to introduce ourselves yet. I'm Vittorio and this is my wife, Carolina, and our children. I hope I'm not disturbing you," Karaoke Man said.

"No, you're not disturbing us at all—at this very moment," Sandra said.

"Thank you," the man replied, seemingly unaware of Sandra's sarcasm.

"It's a little awkward to ask for a favour when we've only just met, but we've got an emergency. We've just had a power cut."

Alfonso feigned surprise. "Oh, really?"

"We've noticed, actually" Sandra said.

"How?" The man sounded genuinely surprised.

"The karaoke stopped."

"You can hear my music?"

"We certainly can," Sandra said.

Karaoke Man smiled as if he had just been paid a compliment.

"There won't be any more music tonight, I'm afraid: the electricity company won't come and fix the problem until tomorrow. We've come to ask for some candles, if you can spare some."

"Of course!" Alfonso replied with a big smile.

Karaoke Man hadn't come to pick a fight or get revenge after all.

"Scented candles would be better," their girl said.

"Sofia!" the mother scolded her.

"We should have some scented candles. I'll find them for you," Sandra said.

She, too, seemed to be warming to their neighbours. Karaoke aside, they seemed quite nice people. They clearly hadn't the faintest idea that their music was causing a nuisance.

"Thank you so much. We'll get you replacements as soon as possible," Carolina said.

"If you have no power, I guess that you won't have any aircon. Would you like some mosquito repellent so that you can sleep with the windows open?" Sandra offered.

"Oh, yes, please," Carolina said.

"We can sleep under the stars. It would be such fun!" her daughter suggested.

"We haven't got anything to sleep on," Vittorio said.

"You could borrow our hammocks," Sandra offered.

"What a marvellous idea! We've got trees to hang hammocks," Carolina said.

"And we've got enough hammocks for you all, if you don't mind that a couple of them are a little frayed," Sandra said.

"Of course not. Thank you so much!"

Once they had waved goodbye, Sandra said to Alfonso, "Our new neighbours aren't as bad as I thought."

***

The following morning, Vittorio turned up at Alfonso's gate. He was pleased to report that the electricity company had reconnected their power without any trouble.

Much to Alfonso's relief, Vittorio was still oblivious to any foul play. But now that power was back on, the karaoke would restart. If

Alfonso repeated his little trick every time, the electricity company and their neighbours would smell a rat.

"Thank you so much for all your help last night. Here are your hammocks. My wife has taken the liberty of mending the frayed edges."

"That's very kind."

"And here are some new candles to replace the ones we used last night. We hope you like lime and lavender. And a new bottle of mosquito repellent."

Alfonso was touched.

"You didn't have to do all this."

"It's the least we could do, after inconveniencing you last night."

"That wasn't an inconvenience at all."

Compared to the karaoke, Alfonso thought.

"And if you ever need anything from us, just ask."

"Thank you."

Vittorio turned to leave when a thought flitted across Alfonso's mind.

"Vittorio, as you're offering, there is actually a favour you could do for us."

Vittorio turned around and smiled.

"Sure. Tell me."

"Could you turn the volume of your karaoke down a bit? And, if I'm not asking too much, perhaps play just a couple of hours a day?

Sandra and I are the sort who enjoy peace and silence. If you don't mind."

Alfonso braced for Vittorio's reaction but his neighbour's face opened into a smile and he patted his shoulder.

"Of course, my friend. I will use my headphones and it will all be completely quiet for you."

"You don't mind?"

"Not a problem. And remember: all you ever need to do is ask."

Vittorio smiled, patted his back and left.

8. A GRACIOUS HOST

August used to be a quiet month at Villa Lingualarga: most couples avoided getting married during the peak of the scorching Sicilian summer. But as Don Pericle's fame as a wedding organiser had spread, the villa's events diary had filled up and some couples had had to choose less favourable months. So now even the mid-August public holiday, *Ferragosto*, was booked.

***

Despite the sweat on their foreheads, the bride and the groom looked happier than ever.

Thanks to Pericle's hard work and that of his staff and contractors, their wedding party had been a success. A last-minute delivery of industrial-sized fans had helped.

"Thank you so much, Don Pericle. It's been a wonderful day," the bride, Dina, told him.

"The day hasn't been wonderful because of me," he replied. "It's been wonderful because you've got each other."

The couple squeezed each other's hands and nodded.

"But you've worked hard to make it wonderful for our guests too. Thank you," the groom, Corrado, said.

Then he slid into the driving seat of the red Alfa Romeo Spider and turned on the ignition.

"Stop!" a shout came from the gate.

It was the son of the neighbouring farmer, running towards them waving his arms.

"What's the matter?" Pericle asked.

The boy stopped in front of them and, hands on his knees, tried to catch his breath.

"Nobody can go anywhere… This road is closed… A wildfire…at the foot of the mountain."

"Has the fire brigade been called?" Pericle asked.

"Yes…They're already there…The police have closed all the roads in and out of Gentini."

If their nearest village was cut off, that meant that they were cut off too: on the other side of Villa Lingualarga there was only sea.

"Will the fire reach the villa?" Dina asked Pericle, glancing around for escape routes.

Pericle licked his finger and held it up.

"So long as the wind doesn't change

direction, it won't."

"Don Pericle, if you look after our guests, I'll take any volunteers with me to see if we can help the fire brigade," Corrado said, stepping out of the car.

In his younger days, Pericle would have jumped at the chance to join the firefighting expedition. But he was no longer physically fit for derring-dos, and anyway it was his job and duty to attend to the guests' needs.

It suddenly dawned on him that the guests would have to stay overnight.

Pericle had never had overnight guests that weren't family or friends, and never in such a large number. The thought of accommodating all these people in Villa Lingualarga gave him a shiver. The seventeenth century villa was his pride and joy. Like a grand old dame, she could not be treated roughly. Would the guests— including families with children—treat her with the care she needed?

But Pericle had no choice. With the only road closed and the nearest hotels well beyond walking distance, Pericle was duty bound to host everyone, and he was determined to do it graciously and generously.

"Certainly," he said to the bride and the groom. "And everyone will be my guest tonight and until they open the road again."

"Don Pericle, this is above and beyond," Dina said.

"It will be my pleasure to have you all here. There's nothing but farmland for miles outside Villa Lingualarga, and you and your guests need somewhere to sleep. Take it as my wedding gift."

***

Pericle instructed the waiting staff to offer cool lemonade and water to all the guests, then studied the list of family units that Dina and Corrado had provided him. Even if he moved into the gardener's cottage where his friend had a spare room, there would still be too many people for the number of bedrooms and beds.

Pericle felt a twinge of regret for offering his hospitality so quickly. But what was done was done, and now all he could do was try and make his guests' stay as comfortable as possible without damage to his beloved villa.

"If we push all the tables and chairs to the side in the banquet hall, we could have any able-bodied young people sleeping on the floor. In this heat, nobody needs blankets so all we need is something soft to lie on. Cushions, yoga mats…" Dina said.

Whatever a yoga mat was, Pericle was sure that he didn't have one.

"I won't have my guests sleep like in a war

camp," Pericle said.

He went on a recce of the bedrooms. Each room was spacious enough to host more people than the beds available, if only he could give them something to lie on...

He rummaged in the storerooms and found some old wool army blankets that could be used as sleeping mats. Pericle chose the room with the four-poster bed and the white lace curtains for the bride and the groom, and made a mental note to leave a bottle of champagne in an ice bucket and some flowers from the garden in a vase.

He proceeded to assign each guestroom to a family unit, then went downstairs to the library, his study, the parlours and drawing rooms. There were plenty of sofas, chaise longues and cushions which could be turned into beds. By the time he had finished his recce, Pericle had ticked off all the people on the list. Success!

***

Pericle had imagined Dina and Corrado would look relieved at the news that all their guests could be comfortably accommodated. Instead, they looked worried.

"We can't sleep on your furniture. They're precious antiques," Dina said she said, gesturing to the clocks on the gilded rococo console, the porcelains in the glass china cabinets and the damasked chairs and sofa.

"Things are precious if they have value, and what value do they have if we don't enjoy having them?" Pericle asked.

This was what he had been repeating to himself for the last couple of hours, each time his generosity gave way to fear and possessiveness.

But Dina didn't look convinced.

"What if someone sleeps on your sofa and dribbles on the upholstery? Even with the best intentions and all the care and attention, it could easily happen. Not to mention what the children could get up to!" she said with a shudder.

Pericle had already considered these possibilities and worried about them.

"We will cover all upholstery with tablecloths," Pericle said.

Thankfully, catering for weddings meant that he had enough napery to cover everything

Dina nodded reluctantly.

Pericle distributed fans to ventilate the rooms and deter mosquitoes, gave out towels and toiletries, and invited the guests to choose a bedtime read from his well-stocked library. When he was satisfied that everyone was comfortable, he said goodnight and crossed over to the gardener's cottage.

The glow of the fire in the distance was abating and the wind had died down, which should help stop the spread of the fire. Hopefully they would open the road first thing in the morning and everyone could go home before Villa Lingualarga suffered lasting damage.

***

That night, Pericle dreamt about the fire. He was running around the villa trying to put out flames with towels and tablecloths. At one point he shook a sooty towel out a window when he noticed that the villa was surrounded by a big moat. He collapsed on the floor in relief, before realising that as the fire was inside the villa, the moat didn't offer any protection but had trapped the fire in.

Pericle woke with a start and with a crick in his neck due to the unfamiliar bed. He didn't feel at all refreshed, but tired and grouchy.

The air smelled of cinders. The wind that had kept the fire away in the night was now blowing towards Villa Lingualarga. With a prick of annoyance, Pericle imagined that the terrace, the balconies and the windowsills would be covered in ash. And as he had left the windows open overnight for the guests' benefit, the ash must have blown inside too.

Grumpily, he got dressed and headed back

to the villa to check on the situation.

As he reached the bottom of the staircase, he heard raised voices and children crying. He followed the sound to the blue room. There, a family of four was arguing over who had pushed the vase that lay shattered on the floor.

"We're very sorry, Don Pericle. We hope it wasn't something special," they said.

"Nothing special at all," Pericle lied, determined to be a gracious host.

He would not tell them that the vase was a present to his family from Queen Margherita during her visit in 1895, nor that he was very sad to see it in pieces. Instead, he reminded himself that the safety of his guests was more important than any vase.

In the corridor, he met a puddle of water soaking into a Persian rug. It came from the nearby bathroom, where the toilet bowl was blocked and had overflown. Someone had tried to flush too much toilet paper. People who lived in modern houses were unfamiliar with the temperamental plumbing of old buildings and didn't treat it with the respect it needed, Pericle grumbled under his breath.

He had better ring the plumber before the blockage caused further damage elsewhere. The plumber's number was in his address book, which he kept in his bedroom. Currently, a grandpa and a grandma were occupying it with their young grandchildren.

Pericle knocked and a little girl opened the door.

"Good morning, Don Pericle. Thank you for letting us stay in your room," she said politely.

Seeing the child's warm smile and the blissful scene of the grandparents reading a book to a child in bed, Pericle recovered his goodwill. It was nice to see that his sacrifices had not been in vain. At least some of his guests would go home with fond memories of their night at Villa Lingualarga, and would remember him as a gracious and generous host.

But then something in the corner of the room caught his attention. A child was rocking on Pericle's beloved rocking horse.

Pericle's skin broke into goosebumps. That horse wasn't any old toy. It had been his play companion all through his childhood and he loved it almost like a real pet. Nobody had ever been allowed to ride it other than him.

Seeing someone energetically rocking it backwards and forwards felt like a desecration. The adult reminded himself that the guests couldn't possibly have known that the horse was special—he hadn't told them. But the child inside him wanted to pounce on the desecrator and pull him off the horse.

What was that white mop on the floor?

Pericle's blood froze. The horse's mane had come off.

Pericle staggered to the nearest chair and sank in it.

This was too much. He should never have allowed these people into the inner sanctum of his life.

"Are you alright, Don Pericle?" the grandma asked, then followed Pericle's gaze. "Oh, the mane has come off. Has it ever happened before?"

Pericle couldn't speak. He just stared at the bald rocking horse with his mouth agape.

The grandpa got out of bed and said in a jolly tone, "Surely nothing that some glue won't fix."

He picked the lifeless mop off the floor and inspected it.

"The glue must have melted in the heat. We should be able to put it back even without glue," he said cheerfully.

He was about to slot the mane back onto the horse's neck, when Pericle found his voice again:

"Just a moment, please. I want to check something."

He had noticed a small label at the base of

the mane. While the mane had been stuck to the horse's neck, it hadn't been visible, but it was now. Pericle read it.

"*Ettore, b. 1935 d. 1940*"

Pericle gulped. Ettore was his beloved pony, who had died when Pericle was only five years old. Pericle had had no idea that the mane of his favourite rocking horse was Ettore's! Tears brimmed in his eyes.

"Sorry, Don Pericle. We'll surely be able to fix it," the grandma said, flustered.

"It's fine, I'm not upset. I'm just moved," Pericle said.

He showed the tag to the couple and explained its significance to him.

If their child hadn't played with the horse, the mane wouldn't have come off and Pericle would never have found out the truth about it.

"Thank you!" he said to the boy.

They easily slotted the mane back into the horse's neck and Pericle, with happy tears in his eyes, watched another five-year-old boy taking his Ettore for a ride. And it felt good.

***

Later that morning, the bride and the groom emerged from their honeymoon suite beaming. A night spent in the fire of love hadn't turned them to cinders like the patch of forest nearby.

The firefighters had managed to contain the

fire and the amount of forest lost was small after all. By lunchtime, the roads were open again and the guests could leave. Everyone was full of gratitude towards Pericle.

"Thank you for turning a disaster into a success," Corrado told him. "Our guests might forget our actual wedding party, but nobody is going to forget spending the night in your beautiful villa, welcomed like family."

"Has anything been damaged?" Dina asked with concern.

Pericle wasn't going to tell her about the shattered vase, the blocked toilet or the rocking horse's mane. None of it had been done on purpose. On the contrary, the guests had done their best to tidy up and clean up after themselves, including the ash off the terraces and balconies. Additionally, one of the guests, who was a plumber, had fixed the blocked toilet.

"All is fine," Pericle said.

Villa Lingualarga had worked hard that night, but wasn't this exactly what she was for? Things were made to serve people, not people to serve things.

Then the boy who had ridden Pericle's rocking horse came up to him.

"Can you please say goodbye to your horse from me?" the little boy asked.

Pericle smiled.

"I certainly will. And he'll be waiting for you to come back and take him on another ride soon."

9. A DROP IN THE BUCKET

Tanino looked down into the water cistern of the holiday home he shared with his friend, Giacomo. It was only one quarter full.

Summer in Sicily always meant water rationing, and Giacomo must have used too much when he had come at the weekend.

"This water isn't going to last us until Friday. You'll have to call the water tanker," Melina remarked, peering over his shoulder.

But Tanino didn't want to call the tanker. Not only did it cost money, but the last time he had called it, the careless driver had squashed his plants with the hose.

"If we're careful, we can easily make this water last," Tanino reasoned.

"Oh, please, don't," Melina begged. "We're going to be left high and dry in the middle of a shower, lathered in soap."

"That won't happen. We won't be having any showers."

Melina's eyes widened.

"It's the height of summer. We're sweaty. We need showers to wash and to cool down!"

"We can dampen our skin with a wet cloth," Tanino argued.

Melina scowled and seemed about to voice her disapproval but didn't. Instead, a smile spread slowly on her face.

"Fine. We shall make this water last," she agreed.

***

Melina had been completely against Tanino's idea until a thought had dawned on her. No water meant no housework.

There would be no laundry, no floor mopping, no bathroom cleaning.

From the moment they had arrived at the cottage, she had been busy washing beddings, mopping floors and wiping windows. She had scrubbed the parasol back to its original bright red, she had wiped the terrace's railings and made the patio's flagstones gleam.

But if she couldn't use water anymore, all the housework she could do would be a little dusting and sweeping. Then this would become a holiday for her, too.

If the price for her rest was a missed shower or two, never mind.

They sat down and drew a list of forbidden

activities. Car washing, floor mopping, garden watering, bathroom cleaning, laundering and showering all went on it.

Then Tanino pushed a magazine in front of her.

"This article has good water-saving tips."

Melina read it. As well as the usual advice about turning taps off when not in use and swapping baths with showers, it also suggested using a cup to rinse teeth, sharing toilet flushes and putting stickers near taps to remind people to turn them off.

The article also recommended that washing-up be done in a bowl rather than under the tap, and the rinse water be used to flush the toilet. Apparently, the pasta's cooking water was an excellent degreaser! Fruit and vegetables, too, were to be cleaned in a bowl, and the rinse water used to water plants.

As she read all this, Melina started doubting if she'd made the right choice agreeing to this plan. Rather than putting her feet up, it sounded as though she would be lugging basins of water round the place all day!

However, it was at bedtime that she regretted her choice most. A refreshing shower was part of her summer bedtime routine. There was nothing like a shower to wash the sweat and dust off her body and cool her for a better night's sleep.

She tried sponging herself, as Tanino had suggested, but it wasn't the same.

She lay in bed awake, listening to Tanino snoring. Unlike her, he had clearly taken their new water-saving regime in his stride.

***

As soon as Tanino woke up the following morning, he went outside and surveyed his vegetable patch.

He hadn't watered it the day before, and it showed. The almond tree had dropped some of its fruitlets, the tomato plants were drooping and the lettuces were so limp that they wouldn't be good even for the caterpillars.

Tanino's heart shrivelled like the leaves he was inspecting. What had been the point of not calling the tanker for fear it would squash his plants, if his plants were going to die anyway? His vegetable patch needed water.

At lunchtime, he went into the kitchen, got the water Melina had used to wash fruit and vegetables and gave it to his plants.

That evening, he returned to the kitchen hoping for more water, but Melina hadn't washed any fruit or vegetables.

"Could we have a salad with our dinner?" Tanino suggested.

"If you can bring me any, yes," she replied.

But the lettuces were still limp after a long hot day, the tomatoes were too small and, unless he drove into the village and made the car dirty, Tanino had no vegetables to bring to the table. No vegetables meant no rinse water, and no rinse water meant no vegetables. In this vicious cycle, all his plants would be dead in a short while.

He padded to the cistern and checked the water level. It had hardly changed. Maybe they could ease their water-saving regime a little.

There must be some water to spare for his plants, surely. He wouldn't use a hosepipe, just a watering can, and only a few drops here and there. It would hardly make a difference to the cistern's water level and Melina wouldn't even notice—especially if he watered the plants at night while she was sleeping.

Plants were best watered in the dark anyway.

***

It was a very hot night and Melina couldn't sleep. A bedtime shower would have really helped.

Earlier that day, she had checked the cistern. The water level had hardly gone down. Surely one quick shower wouldn't have done any harm, but it would have gone a long way to helping her sleep, and she wouldn't be tossing and turning in bed now.

Tanino wouldn't have understood.

What if she showered while he was asleep? He would be none the wiser and wouldn't be upset. It was a great idea.

She waited patiently for the sound of regular breathing and snoring, but tonight it wasn't coming.

A little after midnight, Tanino finally fell asleep and Melina slunk to the shower.

As she turned the tap on, she started counting to sixty, her self-imposed time limit. But the water was so refreshing on her skin that she soon lost count.

When she eventually returned to bed, she had no idea how long she had been in the shower, but she knew that it was longer than she had planned.

Fully refreshed, she still struggled to sleep. Clearly, a clean body with a dirty conscience was no better for sleeping than the other way round.

***

Tanino woke up at the first rays of dawn and was immediately cross with himself.

He had planned to wait for Melina to fall asleep, then go out and water his plants. Instead, he had fallen asleep before her.

Could he still have a chance now? She was snoring away, fast asleep.

He slunk out of bed and tiptoed out to the garden. Looking over his shoulder in case Melina appeared, he filled one, two, three watering cans from the tap and emptied them onto the parched soil with great satisfaction.

But as the water quickly disappeared down the cracks in the earth, he realised that a few watering cans' worth of water were only a drop in a very dry bucket. His plants needed more than that, and he would have to deliver it faster if he didn't want to be found out.

Under the outdoor tap, coiled like a tempting snake, lay the hosepipe.

If he were to use the same amount of water, what difference would it make if he watered the plants with the hosepipe instead of the watering can?

A moment later, water poured out of the hosepipe onto his vegetable patch, darkening the soil.

It was a joy to watch, and he could have happily continued if sounds from inside the house didn't alert him that Melina had woken up.

He hastily turned the tap off and put the hosepipe away, just before Melina emerged onto the patio for her breakfast.

What time was it? The sun was clear of the hills now. How long had he been watering the garden?

Worried, he rushed to the cistern and lifted the lid. There was only half the amount of water there had been the day before. Guilt clawed at him. How were they going to last till Friday with this little water?

***

Melina saw Tanino kneeling by the cistern and peering inside, and her blood ran as cold as last night's shower.

"How are we doing with the water?" she asked nervously.

He shook his head.

"Not good."

She kneeled next to him and peered in. There was very little water. Guilt drowned her: her lengthy shower had caused that disaster.

"I'm sorry," she said.

"It's not your fault," Tanino replied, which made her feel even more guilty.

For a little while they remained kneeling there like two penitents.

***

Tanino decided it was time to call the water tanker.

"Sorry, there are no delivery slots available until next week," they told him over the phone.

That was no good.

Tanino tried another company, but they

were booked up too, and another one was too far and didn't deliver to their area.

"No luck. We'll have to make do with what we've got until Friday," he had to tell Melina.

Guilt swamped him. He had caused this with his reckless watering of the garden, and now his innocent wife was going to pay the price.

"How will we do it?"

"We'll need a more drastic water-saving plan," he said, and promised himself that, this time, he would do his best to make it pleasant for Melina.

"There will be no more cooking," Tanino announced. "We're going to eat at the café in the village every day."

***

Under different circumstances, Melina would have been overjoyed with this news, but not this time.

It was solely her fault that they were forced to have meals out.

Every meal she had at the café, whether it was a calzone, a plate of lasagne or a pizzetta, tasted bitter.

Without any work to do, she idled on the deckchair all day, mulling over her guilty secret, unable to sleep at night.

***

The lettuces had perked up and the tomato

plants stood straight and tall, but Tanino couldn't find any pleasure in them.

What had been the point of saving his plants from drooping if he'd made his wife droop instead? Melina lay on the deckchair all day with a sad look on her face, and it was all his fault.

His secret gnawed at him day and night, until he couldn't take it any longer.

"Melina, I have a confession to make," he told her one bedtime.

"So have I," she replied.

"I hosed the garden while you were sleeping," he said at the same time as she said, "I had a long shower while you were sleeping."

They burst into a chuckle, each relieved not to be the only culprit.

"I forgive you if you forgive me," Melina told Tanino, to which he readily agreed.

Relieved of their guilt, they finally fell into a sweet, deep slumber.

***

The next morning, they were woken up by the whirring of the water pump. It was Friday!

Water rumbled under the ground, gurgled through the pipes and gushed into the cistern.

Still in their pyjamas, Tanino and Melina watched the cistern fill up and thought that there had never been a more wonderful sound than that of running water.

"You can have a shower now," Tanino told Melina.

"And you can water the plants," she returned.

So they did, but they were careful not to use too much water.

And there in the garden, where Tanino had used rinse water from the kitchen—the rinse water speckled with tomato, pepper and basil seeds—were tiny new plants poking up.

10. ONE SUMMER IN SICILY

England was home for Piergiorgio. He had been born there in 1935 and he didn't know any other place.

His parents had immigrated from Italy and had given him a Roman nose, a copper complexion and a name that the locals struggled to pronounce and spell. So, for all his classmates, friends and teachers, Piergiorgio was Italian.

Instead of English nursery rhymes, his mother had told him stories of the Befana. When other mums gave their children Cornish pasties for their packed lunches, Piergiorgio got a square of *pasta al forno*. No matter how much he tried to speak, act and think like his classmates, he was always a little different. A little foreign.

"In Sicily, the sweetest figs grow on the roadsides, tomatoes are red and soft, and lemon blossom fills the air with a wonderful scent," his parents told him. They had no doubt where they belonged. Perhaps Sicily was his home too.

That summer, on his nineteenth birthday, Piergiorgio gathered his savings and bought a train ticket to his parents' hometown of Syracuse.

If there was a place in the world where he wouldn't be a foreigner, it had to be there.

***

Nunzia had known since she was eight years old. The British troops had glided down from the sky to free her land, and a soldier with eyes as blue as the sea had given her a sweet. She had decided then that she would only ever marry a British man.

But when she turned eighteen and it was time to think about marriage, the British troops had long gone.

"Where are we going to find you a British man?" her parents asked her.

"How will you speak to him if you don't know English?" her sister added.

Nunzia didn't know the answers. All she knew was that none of the young men in Syracuse could hold her interest.

She wanted to marry someone different and exciting, who could tell her stories of places and people she had never seen. She wanted someone who came from a faraway land.

"If I can't find such a man, I won't marry at all," she told her family.

***

When the train slowed down into Syracuse station, Piergiorgio couldn't tell which of the people on the platform were his family. Everyone looked like him!

Already, at the Italian border, where the officials had checked his documents and pronounced his name correctly, he had started feeling at home. As the train had travelled down the Italian peninsula, he had seen more and more people like him. For the first time in his life, he wasn't different.

When the train stopped, nobody came to welcome him. Instead, he walked up and down the platform, looking for the relatives he had never met and who had never met him.

It was only when Piergiorgio spotted a man holding a card with his name that he found them, and he was enveloped in hugs.

"You look just like your mother!", "You're all your father!" teary-eyed uncles and aunts declared, pinching his cheeks affectionately.

How glad he was now that, despite his objections, his parents had always insisted on speaking Italian at home! Thanks to that, he could communicate with his relatives and other people. Maybe he'd found a place to call home.

In England, his parents and siblings had been all the family he had. In Syracuse, he had more uncles, aunts and cousins than he could count. He need only take a few steps out on the street to meet someone related to him. He had never felt so connected.

As days passed and meals at Uncle Ciro's house turned from banquets to ordinary affairs, he noticed that the best morsels, special cuts of meat and first fruits of the season were being reserved for him.

As he moved from Uncle Ciro's place to Auntie Rosaria's, then Auntie Giuseppina's, he realised that he was always given the best bed and the newest linen.

His family were doing this with the best intentions but singling him out made him feel less like family and more like a guest. It didn't help that his cousins introduced him to their friends as their "English cousin". Everywhere he went he was "The English man".

Where was his home? Everyone else seemed to know the answer except for him. His home was somewhere else.

Now the dusty Sicilian roads and the parched hills bathed in sun felt alien to him.

***

When Piergiorgio told his relatives that he was

leaving, nobody was surprised. Of course he was going back to his parents.

"Before you go home, we'll take you sightseeing and you must try the local food," his relatives told him.

The next day, they took him to Piazza Armerina, where a Roman villa was being excavated. Beautiful mosaics, pristine columns and frescoed walls revealed the lavish life the wealthiest Romans had enjoyed in Sicily.

The following day, they visited Noto, with its exuberant Baroque buildings left by the Spanish domination. They visited the Arab quarters on the island of Ortigia. There they saw Norman vestiges too, and the remains of a couple of Greek temples, as well as an ancient Jewish bath.

Piergiorgio tried the fried rice balls filled with meat or cheese. *Arancini* had been invented by the Arabs and adopted by the Norman-German King of Sicily, Frederick II, as a packed lunch to take on hunting parties. The idea reminded Piergiorgio of Cornish pasties.

The sweet watermelon jelly had probably originated within the Albanian community in Sicily. The array of sights, smells and tastes was dizzying.

Riding the bus back from Modica, where

they had tasted the local chocolate specialty made according to an Aztec recipe, Piergiorgio turned to his uncle.

"You've shown me Greek and Roman remains, Byzantine and Arab streets, Norman and Spanish monuments. I've tasted Arab and Albanian food. Could you show me something Sicilian too?"

"All the things we've shown you are Sicilian," Uncle Ciro answered.

"But they're foreign," Piergiorgio pointed out.

"If you go back far enough, every Sicilian is a foreigner," Uncle Ciro explained with a smile. "We're the children of the Greeks and the Romans, the Byzantines and the Arabs and all the rest. Even the prehistoric tribes who inhabited Sicily had come from Italy and Iberia. We're an island. Everyone and everything has had to come from somewhere else."

Piergiorgio looked at the olive groves shrouding the sides of the hills.

"How about olive trees? Surely they are as Sicilian as can be."

"Yes, but the Greeks brought them over," Uncle Ciro replied.

"What about lemons? Sicilian lemons are famous all over the world."

"The Arabs introduced them," Auntie

Giuseppina said.

Outside her house, a woman was spreading a tomato paste on a wooden board to dry in the sun and make tomato extract.

"What about tomatoes?" Piergiorgio asked.

"They've come from the Americas."

Sicily had been a melting pot of people, but to some extent, the same must have happened everywhere else. If you went back far enough, everyone and everything had come from somewhere else, so what did it matter if he was English, Italian, neither or both? Home was where he put down his roots.

***

"Tonight is your last night in Sicily and we have a special treat for you," Uncle Ciro told him.

Piergiorgio was speechless when the bus took them to a beautifully preserved Greek theatre.

"We're going to watch one of the Greek tragedies that people watched here thousands of years ago, sitting on the same steps," Uncle Ciro explained.

The thought sent a frisson of emotion through Piergiorgio. It was such a special treat.

Against the backdrop of a spectacular sunset, the actors stood on the same stage where their predecessors performed the same play to an audience two thousand years before.

When the play started, despite the marvellous natural acoustic of the theatre, Piergiorgio couldn't catch the words. The ancient Greek original had been translated into a literary Italian that the local people had learnt at school but he hadn't.

With every chorus, every change of scene, Piergiorgio grew increasingly curious about what was happening. A man was chained to a rock. What had he done wrong?

The girl sitting on the other side of Piergiorgio had a book open on her lap. It was the text of the tragedy they were watching. She was the one to ask.

"Excuse me, can you tell me what's happening in the story?" he whispered to her, trying not to disturb the other spectators.

Her hair smelled of chamomile and vanilla.

"Zeus is punishing Prometheus for teaching mankind how to use fire," she whispered back.

Her voice was the sweetest sound he had ever heard.

All through that act, she kept giving him pointers about the plot, but all he could think of was her. He wanted the play to never end, and the girl by his side to stay there forever.

***

Piergiorgio didn't catch his train the next day. He met Nunzia every day and, the more he got to know her, the more he grew sure that she was the girl for him.

One day he asked her if she would marry him. "I don't fit in anywhere," he warned her. "I'm not Sicilian enough for the Sicilians, nor English enough for the English. Will I be enough for you?"

"You're all that I've ever wanted," she replied, kissing him.

Her parents gave them their blessing, confessing they'd given up hope that their daughter would meet a man of her liking.

But Piergiorgio was everything: English and Italian, different and familiar all in one.

They had a celebratory meal—a Moorish pasta dish of spaghetti with tuna, eggs, pine nuts, orange, lemon and toasted breadcrumbs, followed by a fish soup and watermelon jelly for pudding.

It had been such a delicious and lavish meal that Piergiorgio was surprised by Nunzia's excitement when he shared with everyone some rhubarb and custard boiled sweets he had brought from England.

"Where are we going to set up home?" Nunzia asked him later, when they were alone.

"Wherever you like," Piergiorgio replied with a smile. "Home, for me, will always be with you."

The End

Other books by Stefania Hartley

In this series:

Sweet Surprises
The Season to Be Jolly
To Be Loved
Drive Me Crazy
A Season of Goodwill
What's Yours is Mine
Stars Are Silver
A Slip of the Tongue
Confetti and Lemon Blossom
Fresh from the Sea

Other collections of short stories:

Good Habits
Welcome to Quayside
Tales from the Parish
Keeping It Cool

Romance novellas:

How to Choose a Husband
The Italian Fake Date
Sweet Competition for Camillo's Café
Second Chances at Mamma's Trattoria

Under Far Eastern Skies

Cosy mysteries:

Father Roberto and the Missing Money
Father Roberto and the Runaway Ring
Father Roberto and the Rural Riots
Father Roberto and the Mystery of the
Microscope

ABOUT THE AUTHOR

Stefania was born in Sicily and immediately started growing, but not very much. She left her sunny island after falling head over heels in love with an Englishman, and now she lives in the UK with her husband and their three children.

Having finally learnt English, she's enjoying it so much that she now writes novels and short stories which have been longlisted, shortlisted, commended, and won prizes.

She'd love you to leave a review and to sign up for her newsletter so she can let you know when a new book is out and send you an exclusive short story:

www.stefaniahartley.com/subscribe